LEGO STAR WARS™

GREAT ADVENTURES

BY ACE LANDERS AND ELIZABETH SHAEFER
ILLUSTRATED BY DAVE WHITE

THE REPUBLIC IS IN TROUBLE. THE EVIL SITH LORD DARTH SIDIOUS AND THE GREEDY TRADE FEDERATION ARE PREPARING TO ATTACK. THE ONLY PERSON THAT STANDS IN THEIR WAY IS YOUNG QUEEN AMIDALA OF NABOO.
I CAN'T WAIT TO STEAL THE QUEEN'S JEWELS!
AT LAST I'M HAVING FUN!

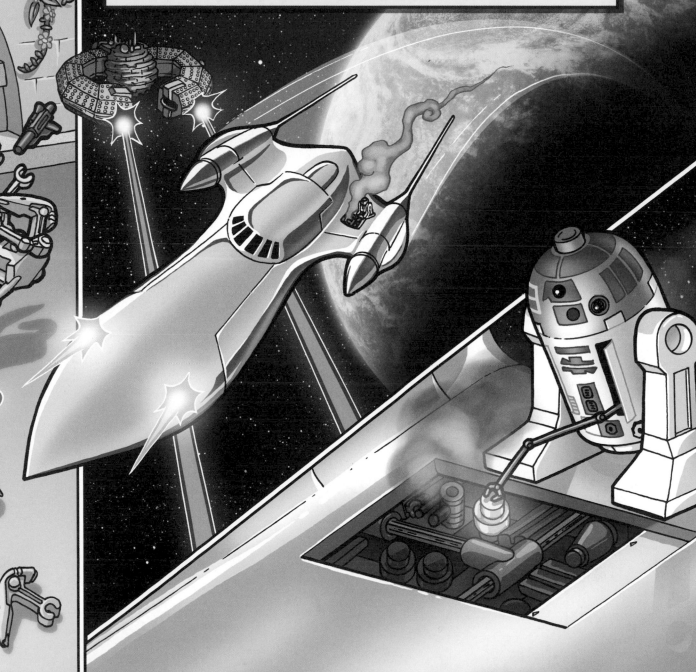

THANKS TO THE JEDI, THE QUEEN BOARDS HER ROYAL STARSHIP AND ESCAPES FROM THE TRADE FEDERATION'S BLOCKADE. WHEN HER SHIP IS DAMAGED, A PLUCKY LITTLE DROID NAMED R2-D2 REPAIRS IT.

WHEN QUI-GON AND HIS TEAM GET BACK TO THEIR SHIP, THEY FIND A STRANGE SIGHT — DARTH MAUI'S PARTY TOWN.

THEIR DUEL IS AS FAST AS LIGHTNING.

DARTH MAUL AND QUI-GON CLASH, DODGE, AND SLASH AT EACH OTHER. THE SOUNDS OF STRIKING LIGHTSABERS SLICE THROUGH THE DESERT AIR.

THE QUEEN FLIES BACK TO NABOO TO FIGHT THE TRADE FEDERATION ARMY, BUT DARTH MAUL IS WAITING FOR HER LOYAL JEDI KNIGHTS.

QUI-GON AND OBI-WAN BOTH ATTACK DARTH MAUL. TWISTING AND FLIPPING THROUGHOUT THE FIGHT, MAUL GIVES OBI-WAN A ROUNDHOUSE KICK AND KNOCKS HIM DOWN. THEN HE KNOCKS QUI-GON INTO A CLOSET, SO HE CAN FIGHT OBI-WAN ONE-ON-ONE.

LOCK

TRAPPED FOR A MOMENT BY A ROW OF FORCE SHIELDS LEADING TO THE POWER GENERATOR, OBI-WAN REBUILDS THE BROKEN DROIDS INTO A SPEEDER BIKE AND CHARGES TOWARD MAUL.

ATTAAACK!

AND FINALLY THE HEROES CAN PARTY.

LEGO STAR WARS™

ANAKIN TO THE RESCUE!

RELEASE THE BEASTS!
IT LOOKS LIKE COOKIES ARE NOT THE ONLY SNACK ON THE MENU. HEH-HEH.
UNFORTUNATELY, THE HEROES ALSO FIND THREE BEASTLY MONSTERS READY TO EAT THEM ALIVE!

OBI-WAN IS ALMOST ATTACKED BY A SIX-LEGGED ACKLAY, BUT ANAKIN TAKES MATTERS INTO HIS OWN HANDS.
CRASH!
TORO! TORO!
I BET THESE WOULD GO GREAT WITH MILK.

OBI-WAN AND YODA BOTH ATTACK COUNT DOOKU.

YOU ARE BOTH STRONG IN THE FORCE, BUT I KNOW OBI-WAN'S WEAKNESS...

THE JEDI ALMOST HAVE HIM CORNERED WHEN COUNT DOOKU ESCAPES WITH A WELL-TIMED PLAN.

TRY THESE DARK SIDE CHOCOLATE COOKIES ON FOR SIZE!

NO!

YUMMY!

TEACH OBI-WAN TO NOT RUIN HIS APPETITE BEFORE DINNER, I MUST.

STAR WARS™

REVENGE OF THE SITH

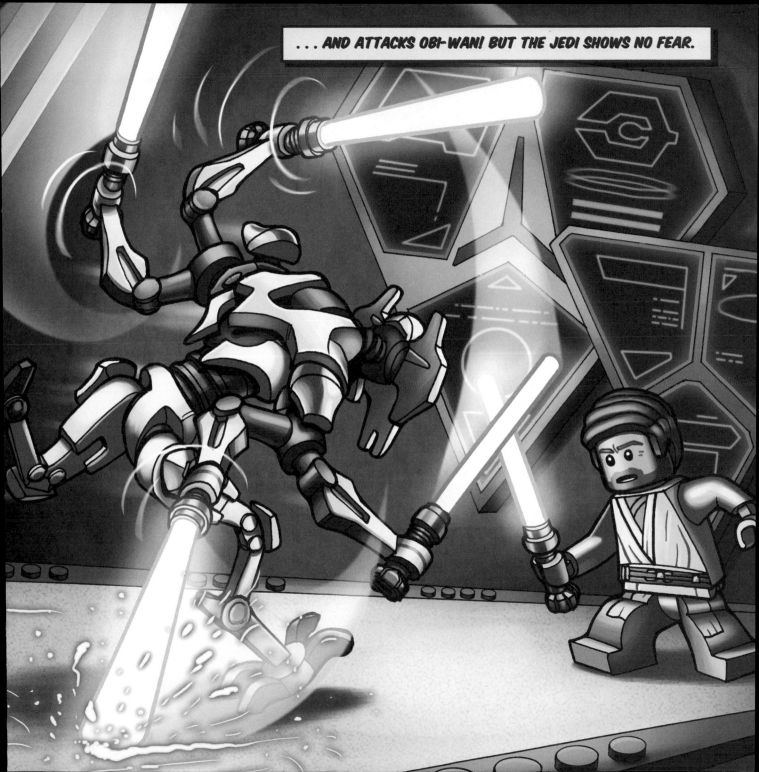

OBI-WAN IS WINNING THE LIGHTSABER DUEL, SO GRIEVOUS TRIES TO ESCAPE AGAIN.
WHY DO THE BAD GUYS ALWAYS RUN? WHY CAN'T THEY EVER JUST GIVE UP?

BACK ON CORUSCANT, ANAKIN RUNS TO SEE HIS NEW BEST FRIEND, PALPATINE, AND TELL HIM THE GOOD NEWS. BUT HE DISCOVERS A SECRET—PALPATINE IS A SITH LORD!
SIR, THE JEDI HAVE WON THE WAR!
JEDI, JEDI, JEDI. THAT'S ALL YOU EVER TALK ABOUT! YOU THINK THE JEDI ARE SO COOL. BUT CAN THEY DO THIS?

WITH ANAKIN JOINING THE DARK SIDE, PALPATINE IS UNSTOPPABLE. FIRST, HE DECLARES HIMSELF THE RULER OF A NEW EMPIRE.
YOU CAN CALL ME EMPEROR!
ORDER 66: A GRILLED JEDI SANDWICH SERVED WITH A SIDE OF WOOKIEE SOUP!
THEN, HE ORDERS THE CLONES TO DESTROY ALL OF THE JEDI IN THE GALAXY.

LATER, ANAKIN TRAVELS TO THE VOLCANIC PLANET MUSTAFAR. THERE, HE IS GREETED BY HIS WIFE, PADMÉ, AND ONE MORE SURPRISE—HIS MENTOR AND ONCE FRIEND, OBI-WAN KENOBI.

THIS IS SO NOT COOL!

YEAH, YOU WERE SUPPOSED TO BE THE CHOSEN ONE!

I'VE CHOSEN THE DARK SIDE! THEY LET ME EAT ALL THE CAKE I WANT!

ANAKIN LOSES THE BATTLE WITH HIS FORMER FRIEND. BUMMED OUT, HE SITS TOO CLOSE TO THE LAVA AND HIS PANTS CATCH ON FIRE. LUCKILY, THE EMPEROR IS NEARBY AND RESCUES HIM JUST IN TIME.
I LIKE MY SITH LORDS ON THE DARK SIDE, NOT BURNED TO A CRISP!
OUCH! HOT! HOT!
SSSSS!

BLACK REALLY SUITS ME.

I KNOW, RIGHT? IT'S VERY SLIMMING.

. . . NAMED DARTH VADER.
WAIT A MINUTE— HOW AM I SUPPOSED TO EAT THIS NOW?!

LEGO STAR WARS™

A NEW HOPE

A LONG TIME AGO IN A GALAXY FAR, FAR AWAY. . . .

The evil Darth Vader was hunting a brave young princess who had stolen the instructions for the Empire's wickedest weapon — the Death Star.

LUCKILY, LUKE AND HIS UNCLE OWEN HAD A VERY SPECIFIC NEED FOR A PROTOCOL DROID. THEY BOUGHT BOTH C-3PO AND R2-D2.

THERE WAS ONLY ONE PLACE ON TATOOINE TO FIND SOMEONE THAT CRAZY: MOS EISLEY. THIS CITY WAS THE ROOTIN'EST, TOOTIN'EST OUTLAW TOWN IN THE GALAXY.
YOU DROIDS AREN'T ALLOWED IN HERE.
WE AIN'T THE DROIDS YOU'RE LOOKING FOR, PARDNER.
BLEEP! BOOP!
THIS NEXT SONG GOES OUT TO THE OUTLAWS IN THE BACK WHO WANT TO DO THE ROBOT DANCE!

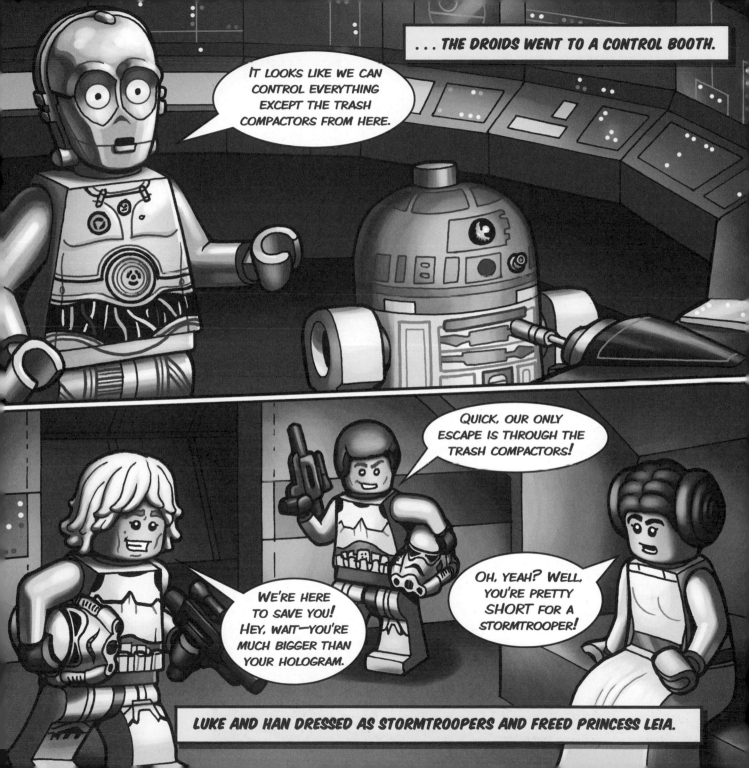

THE X-WINGS STRUCK FIRST, BUT THEY WERE OVERPOWERED BY HUNDREDS OF TIE FIGHTERS. LUKE MANAGED TO DODGE AND WEAVE HIS WAY TOWARD THE DEATH STAR'S ONE WEAK SPOT.

BUT DARTH VADER DID NOT GIVE UP SO EASILY! HE CHASED LUKE AND WAS JUST ABOUT TO BLAST HIM OUT OF THE GALAXY . . .
THERE'S NO ESCAPE NOW.
ARTOO, DUMP THOSE PIECES I'VE BEEN COLLECTING. THEY'RE SLOWING US DOWN.
. . . WHEN LUKE GAVE HIM A SPECIAL SURPRISE!

STAR WARS

™

THE FORCE AWAKENS

REY AND FINN ACCIDENTALLY RELEASE DANGEROUS CREATURES FROM HAN'S CARGO HOLD THAT DISTRACT THE GANGS.
BUT I'M TOO PRETTY TO GET EATEN!

WITH THE GANGS OUT OF THE WAY, HAN TAKES EVERYONE TO MEET HIS OLD FRIEND MAZ. SHE OWNS A BIG CASTLE WHERE ALIENS FROM ALL OVER THE GALAXY COME TO HAVE FUN.

FINN GETS THE CHANCE TO TRY THE NEW WEAPON SOONER THAN HE WOULD LIKE! THE FIRST ORDER TRACKS THE *MILLENNIUM FALCON* TO MAZ'S CASTLE AND ATTACKS.

FINN, BB-8, HAN, AND CHEWIE FLY TO THE RESISTANCE HEADQUARTERS. THERE THEY MEET GENERAL LEIA ORGANA—THE LEADER OF THE RESISTANCE. TOGETHER THEY COME UP WITH A PLAN TO DESTROY THE FIRST ORDER BASE AND RESCUE REY.
I TRIED CALLING. I SWEAR!

ONCE EVERYONE IS SAFE, POE BLASTS THE BASE TO BITS! THE RESISTANCE FIGHTERS RETURN TO THEIR BASE TO PARTY.